# Paris
## in the Rain
### with Jean &
### Jacqueline

14067

# Paris
## in the Rain
## with Jean & Jacqueline

BY
**Thea Bergere**

PICTURES BY
**Richard Bergere**

14067

2-14-64

McGraw-Hill Book Company, Inc.

NEW YORK TORONTO LONDON

Library of Congress Catalog Card Number: 63-14326

Jean and Jacqueline love Paris in the rain.
Sometimes
early in the morning
when they are still snug in their beds
they wake up and hear
the tap, tap, tap
of the rain
beating on their window
and they hurry to dress
to go on an errand for *Maman*.

Médor, their dog,
wants to go too
but they say no.
Minet, the cat,
does not even ask to go.

Up over their shoes
go their rain boots.
Down over their heads
go their rain hats
and—

7

8

Snug under Papa's big umbrella
they hurry out of the house
and around the corner
to the little *boulangerie*
for fresh crunchy rolls
and long golden loaves
of crusty, warm bread.

9

*Bonjour Madame!*
*Bonjour Jacqueline!*
*Bonjour Monsieur!*
*Bonjour Jean!*
Jean and Jacqueline

greet many friends
for the wet shiny street
is filled with people
hurrying and scurrying home
carrying long loaves of bread
beneath their big umbrellas.

After their breakfast
Jean and Jacqueline
walk up and down
and around and around
Paris in the rain.
They like to go
through the little alleys
and narrow side streets
of Montmartre
where they live,
past very old houses
and very high garden walls—

And peek into windows
of small cafés and restaurants
with their clutter
of sidewalk tables
and empty chairs.
They like to watch the artists
painting in the square
and say hello to the flower lady
who sits with her bouquets
under a giant-sized umbrella.

Jean and Jacqueline
like to go down
the steep stone stairways
and then climb up again,
sometimes
all the way
to the top of *"La Butte"*
and the beautiful,
white-domed Sacré-Coeur.

16

17

From the terrace
they can see
the Eiffel Tower
standing tall and bold
against the blue-gray sky
of Paris in the rain.

Jean and Jacqueline
like the hard, heavy rain
that soaks the city
and sends the waters of the Seine
lashing and splashing
to hustle the tugboats and barges.

21

They like the soft misty rain
that washes all the statues
and sprinkles the thirsty flowers
in the market place.

They like the sudden spring showers
that sometimes catch them by surprise
as they walk with *Papa* and *Maman*
in the Luxembourg Gardens.

And in the summer
they like to sail
their paper boats
down the little bubbling brooks
that the rain makes
along each curbside.

On rainy autumn days
Jean and Jacqueline
join their friends
and march to school
two by two
with their bright umbrellas bobbing
like gay mushrooms on parade.

But in winter
Jean and Jacqueline
like to stay warm indoors
and look at the rain
from the window of their cozy room.
They watch it ice the snow-covered houses
and the bare tree branches
and the lampposts
and nip the cheeks of
their friend the *Sergent de ville,*
who waves to them and whistles merrily.
He stamps his feet
and walks back and forth
in the freezing rain.

And best of all—
after *Maman* has kissed them goodnight
and they are drowsy and warm
from their evening baths,
they like to say their prayers, tumble into bed
and then listen to the soft,
tap, tap, tapping of the rain
until it lulls them to sleep.